NOPQRSTUVWXYZ

In loving memory of
Lillian T. D'Amour
(Auntie Lillian)
and her cats:
Holly Su,Tiffany & Baby Barbara

Donated by:
Lisa, Joe & Nicholas Errede

ABCDEFGHIJKLM

Cynthia Rylant

THE COOKIE-STORE CAT

THE BLUE SKY PRESS

An Imprint of Scholastic Inc. • New York

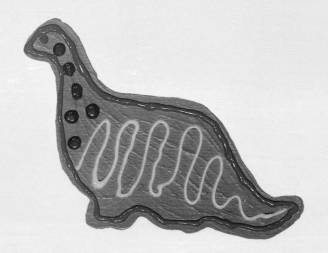

THE BLUE SKY PRESS

Copyright © 1999 by Cynthia Rylant

For information regarding permission,
please write to: Permissions Department,
The Blue Sky Press, an imprint of Scholastic Inc.,
555 Broadway, New York, New York 10012.

The Blue Sky Press is a registered trademark
of Scholastic Inc.

Library of Congress catalog card number:
98-5714

ISBN 0-590-54329-6

12 11 10 9 8 7 6 5 4 3   01 02 03 04

Printed in Singapore   46

First printing, May 1999

Designed by Kathleen Westray

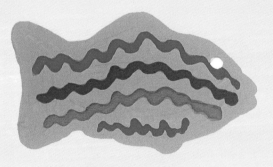

For Carolyn
and her sister Lana,
who know how
to bake a good cookie

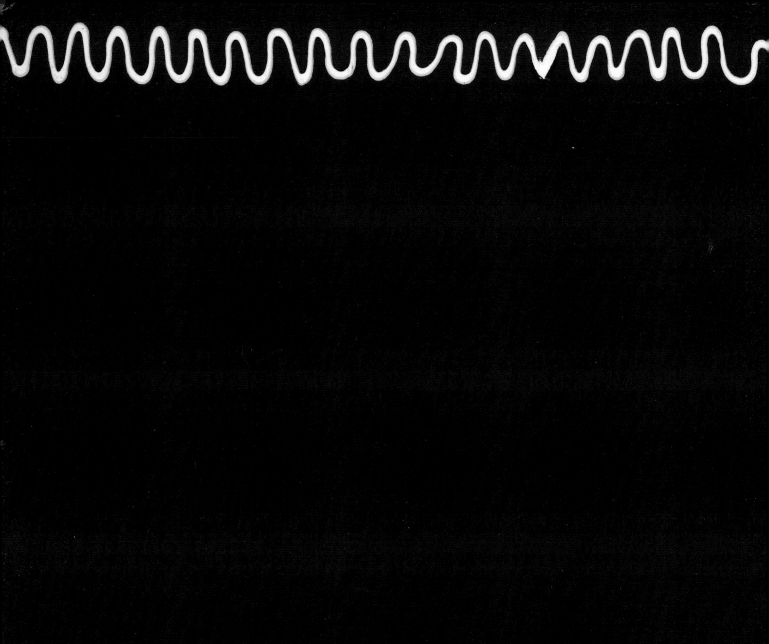

There is a cookie-store cat who spends
his days in the most delicious way.

He sleeps in a little gray bed at the back
of the cookie store and each morning,
around six A.M., the cookie bakers
come to wake him
and kiss him
and tell him
hello.

They tell him he is sweeter than any cookie
they have ever baked.

They tell him he is prettier than marzipan.
They brag that he is a gumdrop gem.

One of the bakers found

the cookie-store cat many

years ago. At six A.M. he was

unlocking the door of his

cookie store as usual when he

heard a thin squeak behind

him. He turned around and

saw two big green eyes in the

tiniest, skinniest, hungriest

kitten's body.

The old baker was a soft-hearted man

and he scooped the kitten up

and carried him inside, where

the bakers fed the kitten real cream

and a bite of cookie dough.

That day they bought a bag

of cat food, and

a little gray bed,

and a white dish

that said "Kitty" on it, and

they made the cat their own.

And now, after so many years,

the bakers cannot remember

ever being without

a cookie-store cat.

Kitty

After the bakers give him his morning kisses each day, the cookie-store cat rises up and stretches and rubs against the bakers' legs as they whip up their orange and maple and mocha frostings. He purrs.

He is a
good cat,
and he
never
jumps
up on
their
baker's
table.

In a little while, he lets himself out through the
wooden screen door painted with cherry drops
and gingerbread men, and he walks along the
street saying good morning to all the shopkeepers

who come early to work. His favorite is the
fish-shop owner, of course, but he is also fond
of the yarn lady and the model-train man. And
he very much enjoys the bookshop people.

After his morning hellos, the cookie-store
cat returns to the place he loves best
of all. He lets himself in through the

wooden screen door and jumps up

to the sunny window to sleep beneath

the chocolate-chip cookie sign.

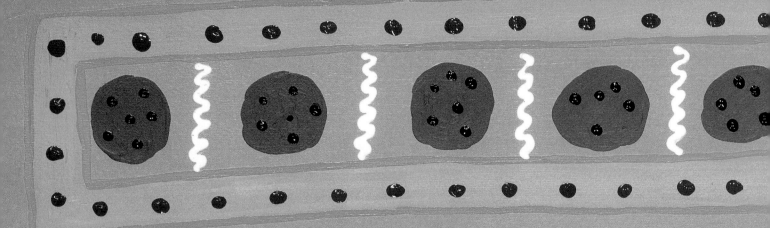

The cookie-store cat has many
friends. Every Monday of every
week, Father Eugene stops by
for a cup of Irish coffee
and three Scotch chewies.
He pets the cookie-store cat
and tells him all about
the new baby in the parish,
or the bingo game he called,
or the old maple in the
churchyard that needs pruning.
The cookie-store cat purrs.
He is a good listener.

After school, every day, the children come. They carry the cookie-store cat on their shoulders and they cradle him like a baby and pass him

one to one, scratching the top of his head as they order up their caramel clusters and ginger creams, their bachelor buttons and frosty fruit squares.

The children sit outside the store with bags of cookies

and boxes of milk, and the cookie-store cat rubs

his nose with theirs, and bats at their pencils,

and licks drops of milk from their fingers.

Christmas is the most wonderful time of all. The bakers wear aprons decorated with candy canes and they fill their shelves with jingle-bell puffs,

snowballs, and chocolate Christmas bonbons. They give away free <u>S</u>anta Claus faces to every child. The cookie-store cat wears a big red bow every day in December and the bell on it makes him jingle when he walks. He is so beautiful and jingles so nicely that he is the talk of the town.

On Christmas Day, when the store is closed, the old baker, the one who found him, comes to have turkey dinner with him.

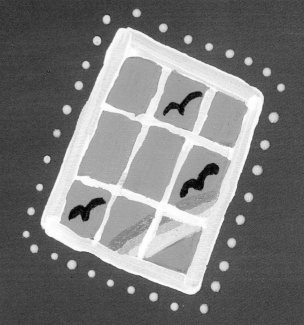

Winter
passes,
and spring,
and summer,
and fall,
and the
cookie-store
cat knows
just where
he belongs.
At the end
of each day,
he knows
that one
of the bakers
will fill a big bag of cookies to take to the Children's
Home, and another will sweep up all of the crumbs

from the floor, and another will wash the fingerprints
from the cherry drops on the wooden screen door.

He knows that the old baker, the one who found him,
will lift up his favorite cat and kiss him and
tell him he is sweeter than a frosted cream,
prettier than a cinnamon sugarplum.

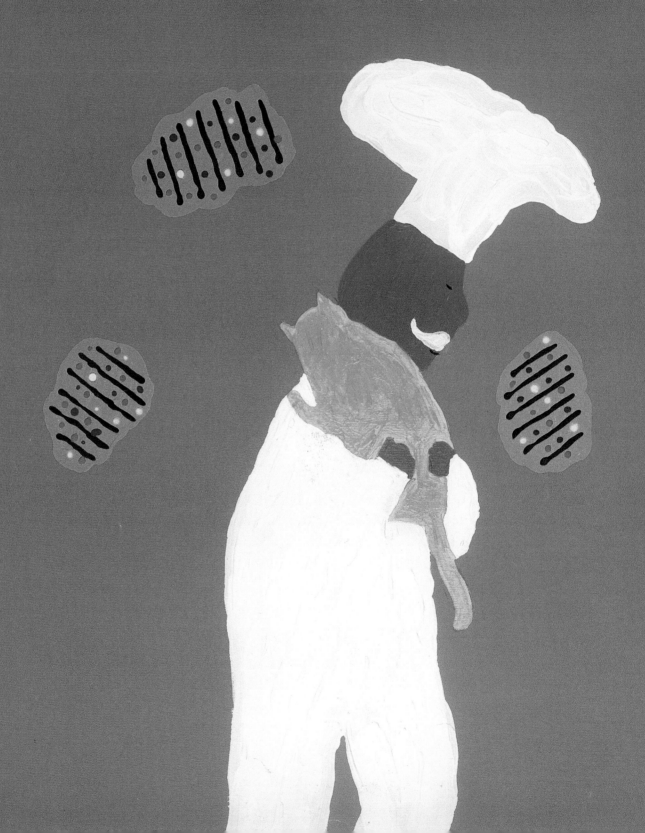

The baker will put

real cream in the

white "Kitty" bowl,

and will carry

the cookie-store cat

to his little gray bed.

Then the old baker and the other bakers will go
home, shutting softly the door behind them,

and the

cookie-store cat

will sleep

in sweet

dreaming

all night long.

And then

of course,

in the morning,

the bakers

will be back.

Gumdrop Gems

1 cup butter, soft
1 1/2 cups confectioner's sugar
1 tsp. vanilla
1 egg
2 1/2 cups sifted flour
1 tsp. baking soda
1/4 tsp. salt
1 cup small gumdrops (no licorice), sliced

Mix butter, sugar, and vanilla until creamy. Add beaten egg. Sift together flour, baking soda, and salt; add to creamed mixture. Shape dough into a roll 2" round, 12" long. Wrap in waxed paper, chill overnight. Cut 1/4" thick slices, place on cookie sheet. Decorate with gumdrop slices.
Bake at 375° for 10 to 12 minutes. Cool.
Makes 48 cookies

Gingerbread Men

1 cup butter, soft
1 cup sugar
1 egg
1 cup molasses
2 Tbs. vinegar
5 cups flour
3 tsp. ginger
1 1/2 tsp. baking soda
1 tsp. cinnamon
1 tsp. cloves
1/2 tsp. salt

Cream butter and sugar. Beat in egg, molasses, and vinegar. Sift dry ingredients, blend into creamed mixture. Chill dough 3 hours. Roll dough onto floured surface. Cut with cookie cutters, place on greased cookie sheet.
Bake at 375° for 5 to 6 minutes. Cool.
Makes 60 cookies

Father Eugene's Scotch Chewies

1/2 cup butter
2 cups brown sugar
2 eggs
1 tsp. vanilla
2 cups flour
2 tsp. baking powder
1/4 tsp. salt
1 cup coconut
1 cup chopped walnuts

Melt butter on low heat. Remove from heat and stir in sugar, eggs, and vanilla. Sift flour, baking powder, and salt. Add to butter mixture with coconut and nuts. Spread in a greased 15" x 10" x 1" pan.
Bake at 350° for 25 minutes. Cut into bars, then cool.
Makes 36 chewies

After-School Bachelor Buttons

3/4 cup butter, soft
1 cup light brown sugar
1 egg
1 tsp. vanilla
2 cups sifted flour
1/4 tsp. salt
1 tsp. baking soda
1/2 cup shredded coconut
1/2 cup chopped nuts
1/2 cup cherries, cut in small pieces

Cream butter and sugar until light and

fluffy. Add egg and vanilla and mix well. Add sifted flour, salt, and baking soda. Mix well. Add coconut, chopped nuts, and cherries. Mix well. Drop from a teaspoon onto greased cookie sheets. Bake at 375° for about 10 minutes. Cool.
Makes 48 cookies

Frosty Fruit Squares

1 1/2 cups flour
1 tsp. baking powder
1/4 tsp. salt
1 1/2 cups quick oats
1 cup brown sugar
3/4 cup butter
3/4 cup fruit preserves
1/2 cup confectioner's sugar

Sift first three ingredients. Stir in oats and brown sugar. Cut in butter until crumbly. Pat 2/3 of crumbs into 11" x 7" pan. Spread with preserves. Top with remaining crumbs.
Bake at 375° about 35 minutes. Cool. Sprinkle with confectioner's sugar.
Makes 24 cookies

Santa Claus Faces

1 1/4 cups sugar
1 cup butter, soft
2 eggs, beaten
2 Tbs. sour cream
A few drops of vanilla
3 1/3 cups flour
1 tsp. baking soda

Cream butter and sugar. Add eggs, sour cream, and vanilla. Sift flour and baking soda, blend into creamed mixture. Chill overnight. Roll dough onto floured surface, cut out cookies with floured Santa Claus cookie cutters.
Bake at 375°, about 10 minutes. Cool, and frost.
Makes 48 cookies

FROSTING

1 cup butter, soft
1 tsp. vanilla
4 cups confectioner's sugar
1 1/2 Tbs. milk
Assorted food coloring

Mix butter and vanilla. Slowly add sugar. Stir in milk. Mix until creamy, adding more milk if needed. Color.

Cinnamon Sugarplums

2/3 cup butter, soft
3/4 cup sugar
1 tsp. vanilla
1 egg
4 tsp. milk
1 1/2 cups flour
1 1/2 tsp. baking powder
1/4 tsp. salt
cinnamon sugar

Cream butter, sugar, and vanilla. Add egg, beat until fluffy. Stir in milk. Sift flour, baking powder, and salt; add to creamed mixture. Drop from teaspoon onto cookie sheet. Flatten with fork, sprinkle with cinnamon sugar.
Bake at 375° for 10 to 12 minutes. Cool.
Makes 48 cookies